I SURVIVED

THE SHARK ATTACKS OF 1916

I SURVIVED

THE SINKING OF THE *TITANIC*, 1912

THE SHARK ATTACKS OF 1916

I SURVIVED

THE SHARK ATTACKS OF 1916

by Lauren Tarshis

illustrated by Scott Dawson

Scholastic Inc.

New York Toronto London Auckland

Sydney Mexico City New Delhi Hong Kong

ISBN 978-93-5275-832-6

Designed by Tim Hall
First printing, September 2010
This reprint edition: June 2024
Printed In India at Shivam Offset Press, New Delhi

FOR LEO

CHAPTER 1

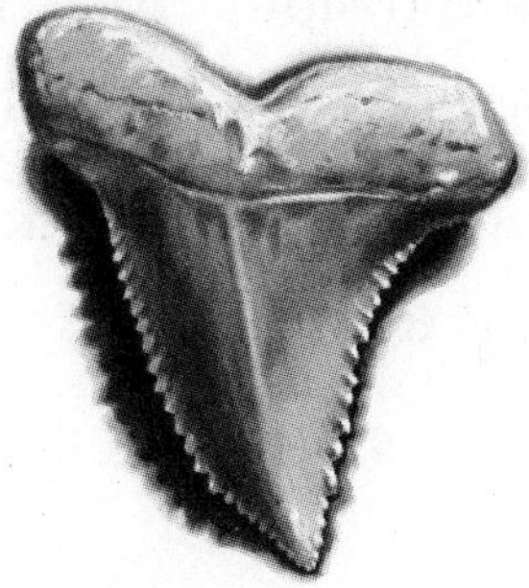

JULY 12, 1916

ELM HILLS, NEW JERSEY

IN THE MATAWAN CREEK

A feeling of terror came over ten-year-old Chet Roscow, a chill deep down in his bones. He had been swimming in the Matawan Creek by himself. But he had the idea that someone — or something — was watching him.

And then he saw it — a large gray fin, slicing

through the water like a knife. What was that? Could it really be . . .

A shark?

That was impossible! Elm Hills was miles and miles from the ocean. How could a shark find its way into this little creek?

There was no way. . . .

But now Chet could see it, coming toward him.

The gigantic shark, bigger than Chet himself. The black eyes staring up through the water.

Killer eyes.

Chet dove toward the shore, pounding through the water, kicking with all his might. His feet touched the bottom. He was running now, looking over his shoulder. The shark was right behind him, its huge jaws wide open, its white dagger teeth gleaming in its bloodred mouth.

CHAPTER 2

NINE DAYS EARLIER . . .

JULY 3, 1916

9:00 A.M.

THE ELM HILLS DINER

The Monday morning breakfast rush at the Elm Hills Diner was finally over.

Chet's feet ached. He was covered in syrup, doughnut crumbs, and bacon grease. His curly red hair was damp with sweat. But he was surprisingly happy. Uncle Jerry was paying him a fortune to help out at his diner this summer—fifteen cents a day! Chet liked being surrounded by familiar faces and hearing folks calling out his name while he worked. Best of all, he was finally making some friends, his first since he came to live with Uncle Jerry last January. He was staying here for the year, while Mama and Papa were in California on business.

Chet was wiping down the counter when the front door banged open.

He smiled when he saw Dewey, Sid, and Monty rushing toward him. They came in every morning on their way to work at the tile factory. Chet had seen them at school—the loud boys who were always talking about baseball. But he hadn't gotten to know them until this summer.

"Did you hear?" Dewey said, his freckly cheeks red with excitement.

"You won't believe it!" said Monty, whose spectacles were fogged up from the humidity.

"Let me tell him!" said Sid, pushing his friends aside. He was the shortest of the three, and always in charge. "It was a shark!"

And then they all started talking at once.

"A shark attack!"

"It was huge!"

"Bit off a man's leg!"

"There was blood everywhere!"

"The man is dead!"

"It happened right in Beach Haven!" said Monty.

Beach Haven was about seventy miles south of Elm Hills, right on the Atlantic Ocean. Chet had heard about the fine hotels there, and the people who swam in the ocean in their fancy bathing costumes. But he'd never heard of any shark attacks!

Uncle Jerry appeared from the kitchen, his bright blue eyes shining and his thick dark hair neatly combed back.

The guys always stood a little straighter when

they saw Chet's uncle. He'd been a baseball legend growing up here in Elm Hills. He could have gone pro, but he'd hurt his knee sliding home in a championship game. The team won, and Uncle Jerry could never play again. He still limped a little after a long day of work.

"What's this about a shark?" he said as he passed out cinnamon doughnuts to each of the boys. "You fellas aren't trying to fool us, are you?"

Chet knew the guys loved to pull pranks. On the last day of school, they'd put a frog in Minnie Marston's lunch pail. She was the prettiest girl in school, but she'd been so mad her face turned an ugly shade of purple.

"We're not foolin'!" Monty said, pulling a rumpled piece of newsprint from his trouser pocket. "Look at this!" he said.

He handed it to Chet. It was from the *New Jersey Herald*. The hair on the back of Chet's

DINER
KILLER SHARK
ATTACKS SWIMMER!

neck stood up as he read the story. Uncle Jerry read it over his shoulder.

KILLER SHARK ATTACKS SWIMMER!

JULY 2, 1916

BEACH HAVEN, NEW JERSEY

Charles Vansant, 25, was attacked by a large shark Saturday, July 1, while swimming in chest-deep water. He and his family were vacationing at the luxurious Engleside Hotel.

Mr. Vansant, known by all as a man of exceptional charm and great promise, was swimming with a dog when the attack occurred. The beach was filled with fashionable ladies and gentlemen enjoying the early evening breezes, when panicked shouts suddenly echoed through the air. A large black fin could be seen swimming toward Mr. Vansant. Onlookers screamed warnings. But it was too late. The shark brutally attacked the young man, who

struggled to swim to shore. A lifeguard and two men rushed to his aid and finally managed to free him from the water.

But he died a short time later of his injuries. This is the first fatal shark attack on a human ever recorded on the northeastern shore of the United States.

Uncle Jerry laughed.

Chet stared at him. His uncle was tough. But did he really think a man getting ripped apart by a shark was funny?

"Boys, that article is a hoax," Uncle Jerry said. "A shark will not attack a human. It's a proven fact. Haven't you ever heard of Mr. Hermann Oelrichs?"

None of them had.

"The guy was a millionaire," Uncle Jerry said. "Owned a big shipping company. One day—let's see, I think it was about twenty-five years ago—this gent was out on his yacht with his rich friends, not far from New York City. They were out in the ocean, and they sailed right into a big school of sharks. The ladies screamed. But Oelrichs put on his bathing costume and dove into the water, practically right on top of those sharks."

"Why did he do that?" Sid said.

"To prove that the sharks wouldn't attack," Uncle Jerry said. "He made a real commotion, splashing and kicking, even shouting at the sharks. And wouldn't you know, the sharks swam away. They were scared as rabbits."

Sid glanced at Chet and smiled.

"And that's not all!" said Uncle Jerry. "Mr. Oelrichs offered a five-hundred-dollar reward to anyone who could come up with one case of a shark attacking a human on the northeastern coast of the United States."

"Five hundred bucks!" said Dewey. "That's crazy!"

"Maybe," Uncle Jerry said. "But nobody ever collected. Because a shark simply will not attack a human. That cherry pie over there is more likely to attack you than a shark is."

They all laughed.

But then a gravelly voice spoke up from the end of the counter.

"You got it wrong. Some sharks are killers."

It was Captain Wilson, who came into the diner every day for breakfast. A long time ago he had been a whaling ship captain. But now he puttered around the creek in his broken-down motorboat. Usually he had a dazed look in his eyes, like he wasn't sure where he was.

But now the Captain's eyes were sharp.

"You've seen some sharks, Cap?" Uncle Jerry said, refilling the Captain's coffee cup.

"Seen one?" the Captain said. "A white shark almost bit me right in two."

"That so?" Uncle Jerry said, winking at Chet.

"I don't want to scare you lads," the Captain said.

"Please, sir!" Monty said. "Nothing scares us."

"We can take it!" Sid insisted.

Chet realized with a happy jolt that the "we" included him.

Uncle Jerry went back into the kitchen, shaking his head.

"All right then," the Captain said, looking around the empty diner. "But gather close. And don't scream too loud. I don't want to upset the other customers."

CHAPTER 3

"The year was 1852," the Captain began. "I wasn't much older than you lads. It was one of my first whaling voyages. Two years at sea, and finally I was heading home across the Pacific."

His voice was low and whispery, like it was coming from someplace very far away.

"Suddenly, the sky turned black. The wind started to howl, and rain poured down. I'll never forget those waves. I thought our ship was going to be tossed to the moon. And the wind! It ripped our ship apart, like it was made of paper. We all went into the water. I grabbed a barrel and somehow I made it through the night. By the time the sun came up, the storm had passed. I was all alone. Just a tiny speck in the middle of the ocean."

"The other men died?" Dewey asked.

But the Captain didn't seem to hear.

"And then I saw the fin."

"The shark?" whispered Monty, edging a little closer to Sid.

"Shhhh," Sid said.

"It circled me for a long while," the Captain said. "Around and around, real slow, like he was toying with me. Little by little, it came closer, and closer. Until I could see its eyes.

"Black as coal," he whispered. "Killer eyes."

The Captain was looking out the window now, like he expected to see that shark with its open jaws pressed against the glass.

“Killer eyes,” he repeated quietly.

It was a minute before he started talking again. The guys waited with their tongues practically hanging out.

“The beast went underwater, and for a second

I thought maybe it'd decided I wasn't worth the trouble. But then something bumped me in the leg. Scraped me bloody! The skin of a shark is rough. You can use it as sandpaper."

The Captain rubbed his leg like it still hurt.

"It came in for the kill with its jaws wide open," the Captain said. "Big enough to swallow me whole. And the teeth. Like daggers, a thousand daggers, all lined up in rows."

The Captain's hands were shaking now.

"I had an old harpoon tip in my pocket. I grabbed it. And I stabbed the shark." He pounded the counter so hard that his coffee mug crashed to the floor. The Captain didn't notice.

"Right in its killer eye," he said.

"You killed it?" Dewey said.

The Captain shook his head. "Oh, no," he said. "But it swam off. Disappeared. It wasn't my time."

Then he stood up and put on his tattered captain's hat.

"I must get home now," he said. "My sweet Deborah will be waiting for me."

Deborah was his wife. She'd been dead for at least twenty years.

Chet and the guys watched him leave.

Uncle Jerry had come out of the kitchen when he heard the crash of the Captain's cup.

"Poor old guy," he said, as he swept up the mess. "His mind is like Swiss cheese."

"You mean that story isn't true?" Monty asked.

Uncle Jerry shrugged. "I think the Captain spins a mighty fine tale."

"Stabbed it with a harpoon tip!" Dewey laughed.

"Killer eyes!" Monty barked.

"Next the Captain will be telling us he got gobbled up by a whale," Sid said.

Still, Chet thought about the Captain all day. He didn't really believe the story either. Uncle Jerry was right. Whoever heard of a shark attacking a person?

No, it wasn't the shark that scared him. It was the idea of being alone in the middle of the ocean. Strange, but Chet could imagine that feeling. He'd been traveling around the country with Mama and Papa most of his life. Papa was always chasing some new business idea. Selling motorcars in Oregon. Building bicycles in St. Louis. Taking family portraits in Philadelphia. Mama would get them settled into an apartment or a run-down little house. Chet would try to make friends. And just when they were starting to get comfortable, the business would go bad or Papa would get some other idea. "We're hitting the road," Papa would announce. And Mama would have to start packing again.

Chet was supposed to go along to California,

where Papa was sure he'd finally strike it rich. But then Mama decided that Chet would stay with Uncle Jerry instead.

"It's a nice town," Mama had said. "And Uncle Jerry will take good care of you."

Chet remembered all the fun he used to have with Uncle Jerry when he was little, how Uncle Jerry had taught him how to throw a baseball. But they hadn't seen each other in years. Would his uncle even recognize him after all this time?

He shouldn't have worried. Uncle Jerry was standing on the train platform when Chet got off, a huge grin on his face. "It's about time," he said to Chet, wrapping him up in a hug that went on until after the train pulled out of the station. From that first day, Uncle Jerry made him feel right at home.

But Chet missed Mama and Papa. And it didn't matter how much he loved being with Uncle Jerry, or how many people shouted

"Hiya, Chet!" when they came into the diner. Soon enough he'd have to join Mama and Papa in California.

Would he ever really belong anywhere?

Or would he always be on his own, a tiny speck in the middle of the ocean?

CHAPTER 4

That next week was so hot, horses were fainting up and down Main Street. By Thursday, the temperature inside the diner was 102 degrees. But Chet didn't mind the heat. Something amazing had happened that day: The guys had invited Chet to go swimming with them at the creek.

All week they'd been coming into the diner earlier and earlier, and then sticking around even after they'd wolfed down their doughnuts.

"You ever seen the Pacific Ocean?" Sid had asked one day.

"Sure," Chet said.

"What's it look like?" Monty asked.

Chet took a minute to picture it. He didn't want to disappoint the guys.

"A little bluer than the Atlantic. Waves a little bigger maybe. But otherwise just lots of water and waves."

They all seemed satisfied.

"How about the Mississippi River?" Dewey had asked the next day. "You seen that too?"

Chet told them it was wide and muddy.

"I was on a steamboat that got stuck in the mud," Chet said. "We had to stay there for a whole day and night."

That impressed them all.

"You're the luckiest kid I know," Sid pronounced.

"Me?" Chet said.

"Sure!" Monty said. "To see all those places!"

"I don't know," Chet said. "I hate moving around so much."

Hearing those words startled Chet. He felt that way, but he'd never said it out loud. Not even to Uncle Jerry. He hoped the guys didn't think he was bellyaching.

"Hey, why don't you ever come down to the creek?" Sid said.

"We're always looking for you there," Monty said.

Chet tried to hide his surprise.

"It's not the Pacific Ocean," Dewey said. "But it's pretty nice."

"I hear it's better than the Pacific," Chet said.

The guys all laughed.

"Why don't you come today?" Sid said, and of course Chet said he would meet them after work.

Uncle Jerry drew Chet a little map so he wouldn't get lost—a dotted line to the end of Main Street, and then behind the tile factory. Down a steep hill and across a path.

Chet made it to the bottom of the hill, and for a second he thought he was lost. He couldn't see the creek, just tall golden grass. But then he could hear shouts and splashing. He walked through the grass and into a clearing. The guys' dusty trousers and shirts were laid across some low branches. Three pairs of scuffed-up boots were tumbled across the dirt.

And just beyond, there was the creek.

The guys were right: It wasn't much—maybe twenty feet across. He couldn't tell if it was deep enough to dive. But it was nice and shady, and at that moment there was no place on earth that Chet would rather be.

"Hurry up!" Dewey shouted. "The water's perfect."

Chet threw his clothes off and climbed up onto the broken-down dock.

"Jump!" Sid said.

With a running leap, Chet launched himself into the air.

Whoosh! The cool water rose up around him. All of his worries washed away.

The guys gathered around him. Dewey threw a pink rubber ball high into the air.

"Chet! Catch!" he said.

Chet squinted up into the sun and, miraculously, caught the ball.

"Here!" Sid yelled, jumping up and waving his hands. Chet threw the ball, straight enough, like Uncle Jerry had taught him. Sid made a clean catch.

They played ball, then they took turns jumping off the dock and chasing each other back and forth across the creek.

When they got tired of swimming, they sat on

the bank under a big elm tree. Dewey's mother had packed him three big molasses cookies, and the guys fought over who could share with Chet.

"So?" Sid said. "You like it here okay?"

"The creek's nice," said Chet with a mouth full of cookie.

"No, Elm Hills," Monty said.

"You think you'll be staying a while?" said Dewey.

Chet swallowed hard. Just the day before, he'd gotten a letter from Mama. *"We have a nice apartment with a room just for you,"* she wrote. *"I think Papa is going to have some good luck this time."*

"I hope," he said.

The guys all nodded.

"Minnie Marston's sweet on you," Dewey said.

"Really?" Chet squeaked.

"Sure," Monty said, sounding a little jealous. "She told my sister."

They sat there a while, talking about Minnie, and Uncle Jerry's no-hitter in the high school finals of 1908. Then Sid stood up and dove back into the water. They all followed him.

Sid went swimming down the creek, and Chet played ball with Dewey and Monty. He and Monty tossed the ball back and forth a few times.

"Dewey!" Chet called, ready to throw the ball.

But Dewey didn't look at him. He was looking at something downstream. He had a strange look on his face.

And then Chet saw it too: a gray triangle sticking up through the water, heading right for Dewey.

What was that?

It looked like the fin of a giant fish. Was it . . .

He shook his head. His eyes were playing tricks on him.

A shark in the creek was impossible.

He even tried to laugh. His mind must be messed up because of the Captain's story.

But the fin was getting closer to Dewey. Faster, faster, closer, closer.

"Dewey!" Chet shouted.

But it was too late.

There was a huge splash. And then Dewey disappeared.

CHAPTER 5

Chet ran screaming out of the water. "Dewey! Dewey!"

He made it to the bank and searched the water for Monty and Sid, but they were gone too.

They'd been eaten! Chet was the only one left! He was about to run up to Main Street for help, but then Dewey came up sputtering.

"You idiot," Dewey said, looking around. "You kept me under too long! That wasn't the plan!"

Who was Dewey talking to? And what did he mean about a *plan*?

Sid came up out of the water, gasping for breath. Where was the shark? And why was Sid laughing?

"We got you!" Sid shouted at Chet. He held something up.

A chipped gray tile.

The fin.

Chet's head started to spin. He felt like he might throw up. They'd tricked him!

Monty was standing on the bank on the other side of the creek. "I can't believe you fell for that!" he laughed.

Chet couldn't talk. His heart seemed to be stuck in his throat. Why would they do that?

"You should have heard yourself!" Monty shouted. "You screamed so loud! Your mama probably heard you all the way in California."

Chet's cheeks were bright red. His hands were shaking. How could he have thought these guys wanted to be his friends? They just wanted someone to pick on. That was the only reason they'd invited him to the creek.

Chet grabbed his clothes and got dressed.

"Hey!" Sid yelled. "Don't be sore!"

They all scrambled out of the water and ran over to him.

"We were just joking around with you!"

"We didn't mean to scare you so bad."

"We always do pranks!"

But Chet wasn't listening. His heart was pounding and his cheeks burned. He laced up his boots, stood up, and stormed away.

CHAPTER 6

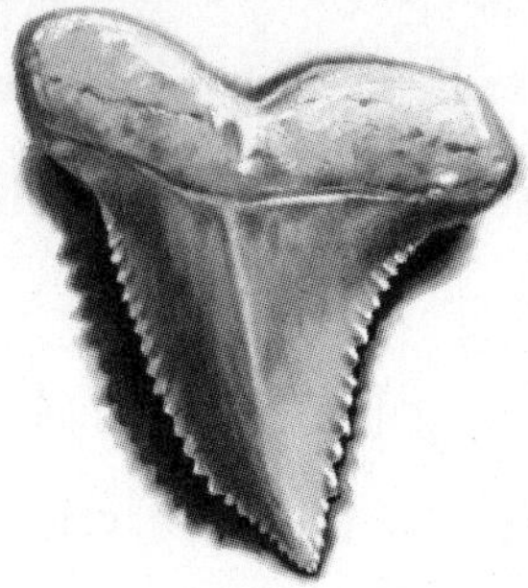

The next day the guys came by the diner, smiling like everything was normal. Chet didn't wave back. He slipped into the kitchen before they sat down at the counter and didn't come out until they were gone.

After the breakfast rush was over, Uncle Jerry handed Chet a mug of root beer and told him to have a seat.

"What's wrong, kiddo?" he asked, sitting

on the stool next to Chet's. "I see you've been avoiding your buddies."

"They're not my buddies," Chet said. "I hardly know them."

Uncle Jerry peered at Chet. "Is this because of that stunt at the creek?"

"You heard about that?" Chet said.

Uncle Jerry chuckled, but not in a nasty way. "They didn't mean any harm," he said. "You should be flattered."

"How's that?" Chet said. "They made me feel like an idiot."

"It means they like you, that you're one of them," Uncle Jerry said. "Now they're expecting you to get them back. Didn't you know that's how it works?"

How could Chet know? He'd never had any real friends before. He wanted to know more. But before he could ask, Mr. Colton and Dr. Jay came through the door. They were Uncle

Jerry's oldest friends. Mr. Colton owned the hardware store. Dr. Jay took care of practically everyone in town. They came in every day for coffee and to chat about baseball with Uncle Jerry.

But today the men didn't want to talk about Babe Ruth's pitching record. Mr. Colton held up the morning paper so Uncle Jerry and Chet could read the front-page headline.

SHARK KILLS SECOND BATHER IN NEW JERSEY

JULY 7, 1916

SPRING LAKE, NEW JERSEY

A shark attacked Charles Bruder, 28, while he was swimming alone in the ocean yesterday afternoon. Lifeguards rushed to his rescue, but the young man's wounds were so severe that he bled to death before they reached shore.

Bruder, a well-liked bell captain at the Essex

and Sussex Hotel, was known to be a strong swimmer. But he was no match for the beast, which attacked without mercy. Before he perished, Bruder was able to tell a remarkable story to his rescuers.

"He was a big gray fellow, and as rough as sandpaper," Bruder said. "I didn't see him until after he struck me the first time. . . . That was when I yelled. . . . I thought he had gone on, but he only turned and shot back at me [and] . . . snipped my left leg off. . . . He yanked me clear under before he let go. . . . He came back at me . . . and he shook me like a terrier shakes a rat."

Bruder tried to say more, but he became too weak. He died of massive blood loss and shock before lifeguards could get him back to the shore.

Officials are warning people not to swim alone.

"I still don't believe it," said Uncle Jerry. "Someone is cooking up these stories to sell newspapers."

"Could be," Mr. Colton said. "Folks are terrified, though. My wife's cousin lives out there, and she says nobody will go near the ocean. They have fishermen out with rifles shooting at anything that moves."

"You know what this reminds me of?" Dr. Jay said. "The Creek Devil."

"What's that?" Chet asked.

Mr. Colton and Dr. Jay chuckled. Then Mr. Colton shifted his hefty body forward on the stool. He leaned closer to Chet.

"Old-timers say there's a monster that lives down near the creek. He's covered with mud. Eats snakes and bats and makes a terrible hissing sound. Moans, too. Legend is that he comes out every decade and drags a kid back into the mud with him."

"People believe that?" Chet said.

"Everyone in town knows the legend," Uncle Jerry said, "but nobody really believes it."

"Except for Jerry here," Dr. Jay said, slapping Uncle Jerry on the shoulder. "When we were little, he wouldn't go near that creek!"

"Bah," Uncle Jerry said, waving his hand at Dr. Jay. "I don't know what you're talking about. Doesn't someone need a wart removed or something?"

Was Uncle Jerry blushing?

Imagine Uncle Jerry being afraid of a made-up monster! Chet smiled to himself. Maybe there was hope for him yet.

Suddenly Chet had an idea for the greatest prank ever. Folks would be talking about it for years. And then he'd be part of the gang for sure.

Dewey, Monty, and Sid were going to come face-to-face with the Creek Devil.

CHAPTER 7

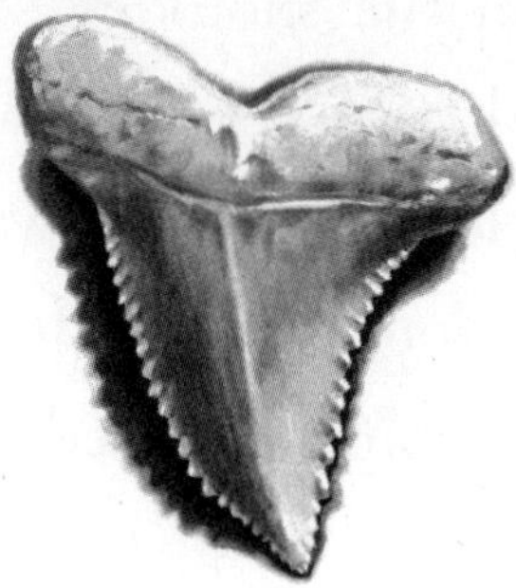

At church on Sunday, Chet went out of his way to say hi to the guys. They seemed relieved that he wasn't mad anymore. And the truth was, he really wasn't, now that he understood how it was with pranks—and now that he had a genius plan for getting them back.

"Come swimming with us today," Sid called as he helped his mother into their buggy. "We'll be there right after lunch."

"Sure!" Chet called back. "I'll meet you!"

Uncle Jerry patted him on the back.

"That's the way, kiddo," he said. "There's no room in a small town for grudges."

Chet was dying to tell Uncle Jerry about his idea. But Chet kept his mouth shut, worried that his uncle might tell someone and spoil the plan.

He saw Minnie Marston as he was leaving the churchyard. She waved to him and smiled, like she wanted him to go up and talk to her. For months last spring Chet had prayed that Minnie would look in his direction. But now? He didn't have time for girls, not even Minnie. He had to get to the creek before the guys. He waved to Minnie and headed home.

Uncle Jerry was going to the diner to take care of some bookkeeping, and Chet headed home to change. He grabbed the bag he'd packed that morning. Inside was a bottle of ketchup, one of his old work boots, and the white cap he always wore at work—everything he needed.

He hurried to the creek, which was completely quiet, and went straight to work.

His plan had two parts. First, he wanted to make the guys think he'd been attacked and dragged, bloody and screaming, into the creek. He dribbled some ketchup along the dock—a trail of blood. He put his boot in the middle of the dock and covered it with ketchup. He did the same to his cap.

Chet stood back and admired his work.

So far, so good.

Now Chet took off his undershirt and trousers and kicked off his boots. He hid them in the tall grass. Then he went to the wettest part of the bank. He scooped up handfuls of the slimiest mud he could find and smeared it onto his face, his arms, and his chest. He used extra mud to cover his head so that no hairs poked through. He had no idea what the Creek Devil was supposed to look like, but he was pretty sure it didn't have orange hair.

Chet was just finishing when he heard voices.

The guys!

Chet closed his eyes and took a deep breath.

Then he let out the biggest, loudest scream he could muster. He screamed like he was terrified, like he was in agony. And then he splashed loudly into the creek, careful not to wash off the mud. He screamed some more, and then waded into the reeds and hid.

"Chet?" Sid called. "That you?"

Chet didn't answer. He couldn't see the guys, but he heard their heavy breathing and their panicky voices.

"Where is he?"

"Is that his boot?"

"What the . . ."

"Oh, my God," Sid whispered. "Is that blood?"

Chet held his breath. Would they really fall for it? Could this actually work?

"Chet?" Sid called. "Chet, you there?"

Chet had to puff up his cheeks to keep from bursting out laughing.

"Isn't that Chet's cap?" Dewey whispered.

A few seconds went by.

"What's happening?" Monty said quietly.

They were falling for it! Now it was time for part two.

Chet gave a low hiss, remembering what Mr. Colton had said about the sound the Creek Devil made before an attack.

"What the heck was that?" Dewey said, his voice shaking.

"Quiet!" Sid said.

"Should we go get someone?" Dewey said.

"HISSSSSSSSSSSSSSSS."

Chet was impressed by how spooky he sounded. Next he started to moan, low at first, and then louder.

"OOOOOOMMMMMMMOOOOOO."

He poked his head through the reeds, not all

the way through, just enough for the guys to catch a glimpse of a hideous head covered with black slime.

The guys stared with bugged-out eyes and wide-open mouths.

"Ahhhhhhhh!" they screamed.

Dewey went tearing away.

"OOOOOOMMMMMMMOOOOOO!"

"AHHHHHHHHH!" screamed Sid and Monty.

They turned to run, and that's when Chet leaped out of the water.

"Got you!" Chet shouted.

Sid and Monty stopped short. Their faces were dead white.

"I got you good!"

He waited for their terrified faces to melt into smiles, for them to laugh their heads off and tell Chet he was a genius.

But they didn't.

Sid stomped onto the dock. He leaned close

to Chet, his face all twisted up and furious. His fists were clenched.

Chet jumped back. Was Sid going to deck him?

Monty pulled him away. "He's not worth it," he said.

"You're an *idiot*!" Sid growled. "We really thought something bad happened to you!"

"How could you think that would be *funny*?" Monty said.

The words came at him hard and cold.

Sid glared at him a few more seconds. And then they turned and walked away.

Chet stood there in shock.

His prank had worked better than he could have imagined.

But it was all wrong.

And here he was, covered with stinking mud, all alone.

CHAPTER 8

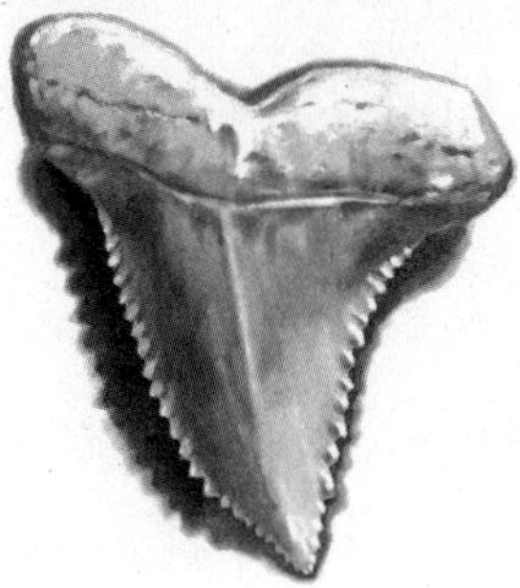

Chet scrubbed himself off in the creek and went back to Uncle Jerry's cottage.

It was too hot to be inside, so he sat on the porch. He sat there a long time. He wondered what Mama and Papa were doing. He pictured Mama, with her soft smile and laughing eyes. And Papa, who always woke up with a happy face, even when they were out of money and had to pack up to start all over again.

Why had they left him here?

He was so deep in his gloomy thoughts that at first he didn't see Uncle Jerry hurrying up the walk.

"There you are!" he said, catching his breath. He sat down next to Chet.

"I thought you were going to be at the diner all day," Chet said.

"I was," Uncle Jerry said, fishing in his pocket for his pipe. He struck his match on the floor, lit the pipe, took a few puffs, and then settled back.

They didn't say anything for a few minutes.

"So there was some excitement at the creek, I hear," Uncle Jerry said.

Chet's heart sank into his boots.

"Poor Dewey came running down Main Street in his drawers," Uncle Jerry continued. "He was screaming about the Creek Devil. His mama called Dr. Jay."

Chet sighed. He didn't look at Uncle Jerry. He'd probably already sent a telegram to Mama and Papa, and was getting ready to ship Chet directly to California. Chet couldn't wait to start packing.

"I went too far," Chet said.

"I guess you did," Uncle Jerry said.

Chet took a deep breath. A spider scurried across the floor and disappeared into one of the cracks. Lucky spider.

There was a strange sound. Chet looked at Uncle Jerry, whose face was beet red. Was he choking on his pipe smoke?

No. He was laughing! His laughter exploded through the air. He pounded his chest a few times. "Sorry," he said through his guffaws. "But that look on Dewey's face . . ." He leaned forward, slapping his leg, shaking his head. "It was a good one," Uncle Jerry sputtered. "Maybe a little too gruesome. But darned good."

Chet wanted to laugh along with Uncle Jerry. But he kept thinking of that furious look on Sid's face when Chet came out of the water.

Monty was right. Chet wasn't worth it. He wasn't even worth a punch in the nose. He had ruined everything!

Tears ran down his face. He turned away from Uncle Jerry, but it was too late.

Uncle Jerry stopped laughing and put his hand on Chet's shoulder. He waited for Chet to stop crying.

What a fool he was, blubbering like this! Over a stupid prank.

"It's all right," Uncle Jerry said.

"No," Chet said, standing up. "I need to leave."

"Where are you going?" Uncle Jerry said.

"To California," Chet said.

Uncle Jerry stared at him.

"I don't belong here," Chet said.

"The heck you don't!" Uncle Jerry said. "You belong here. Like I knew you would. Why do you think I begged your mama to let you stay with me?"

"But I thought Mama asked *you*," Chet said.

"Are you kidding? I've been begging for years. I wrote about a hundred letters, a few telegrams too."

"Why?" Chet said.

Uncle Jerry looked at Chet like he'd asked for the answer to two plus two.

"I thought maybe you were tired of moving around so much," Uncle Jerry said, pulling Chet back down to sit next to him on the porch step. "And there's another reason. You and I are buddies, kiddo. Always were. I was lonely without you all these years."

Chet almost laughed. With all the people who loved Uncle Jerry, who crowded around him every day at the diner, who laughed at his jokes and listened to his stories, how could he be lonely?

Yet Uncle Jerry's eyes, usually all crinkled up and merry, were big and serious. He meant it.

"Did I ever tell you what happened after I

hurt my leg?" Uncle Jerry said. "I moved to New York City. I quit this town. I just wanted to get lost. I couldn't stand the way people looked at me here, like they pitied me. Or like I'd let them down by not becoming a big baseball star."

"Mama never told me that," Chet said.

"Well it's true. But you know what? I missed this place. And I'll tell you what I learned: A person has to face up to things. You never solve anything by running away."

Chet knew Uncle Jerry was right. But how could Chet stay here with the guys hating him so much?

Uncle Jerry seemed to read his thoughts. "You'll find a way to make it up to those friends of yours," he said. "I know you will."

CHAPTER 9

The next two days at the diner, Chet kept waiting for the guys to come in. Every time the door opened, he looked up, hoping to see them elbowing each other to be first to the counter.

They never even walked by.

Chet kept trying to work up the nerve to go and find them, and finally on Wednesday he was ready. It was another scorching day, the hottest yet. After the lunch rush was over, Uncle

Jerry decided to close the diner early. All the ice in the restaurant had melted. The milk had curdled. You could just about cook a flapjack on the kitchen floor.

"I'm going home to stick my head under the water pump," Uncle Jerry said. "Then I'm going to swing in our hammock until the sun sets."

Chet said good-bye to Uncle Jerry and headed for the creek, sure he'd find the guys playing ball in the water.

But the swimming hole was quiet.

Chet realized they were still at the factory. Their shift wouldn't be over for an hour.

While he was waiting, he noticed that there were still splotches of ketchup on the dock. They looked even more like blood now, like evidence of a gruesome crime. He decided to try to clean them before the guys got here, to erase all reminders of his prank. He undressed and jumped into the creek. Then he splashed water up onto the dock, hopped out of the water, and scrubbed the stains with a handful of leaves.

It took three rounds of splashing and scrubbing to clean it up.

By then Chet was so hot that he decided to take a longer swim.

It was peaceful here without everyone splashing and shouting. He floated on his back under the trees, remembering how Papa had taught him to swim in the Mississippi, how Mama sat on the banks waving and clapping.

He had turned to swim back to the dock when—*crash*, he hit something under the water.

Or something hit him.

Hit him so hard in the chest he couldn't breathe.

What was that? An old dock plank? A snapping turtle? Had Sid sneaked up on him and smacked him?

The water around him looked funny, like it was filled with red smoke.

Chet looked down in shock. His entire chest was scraped and oozing blood. What could have done that to him?

A cold terror rose up inside him. He suddenly had the feeling that someone — or something — was nearby, watching him.

And then he saw it.

A gray fin.

It glistened in the bright sun as it glided slowly toward him.

He had to be seeing things. Or could this be another prank? Were the guys getting him back?

But no, this was no tile.

As it got closer, Chet could see the dark shape of an enormous fish, bigger than him. Even bigger than Uncle Jerry. Two black eyes peered up through the water.

Chet's heart stopped.

Killer eyes.

Chet took off toward the shore, pounding through the water, kicking with all his might. Finally his feet touched the bottom. He was running now, his heart hammering, a voice booming through his mind. *Get out of the water! Get out of the water! Get out of the water!*

Almost there—just a few more steps!

He dove forward, landing hard in the dirt. He rolled onto his side and stared in disbelief: It was a shark, a massive shark—dirty gray on top and pure white underneath. Its jaws snapped open and closed. The teeth, jagged and needle sharp, were bigger than Chet's fingers, lined up in rows and curving inward. The shark thrashed, as if it was trying to push itself up onto the bank. Chet wanted to get up and run. But he was frozen to the ground.

Those killer eyes stared unblinkingly at Chet.

And then, with a flick of its tail, the shark thrust itself backward into the water.

It hovered for a second on the surface.

Then, with a *whoosh* of its tail, it disappeared back down the creek.

CHAPTER 10

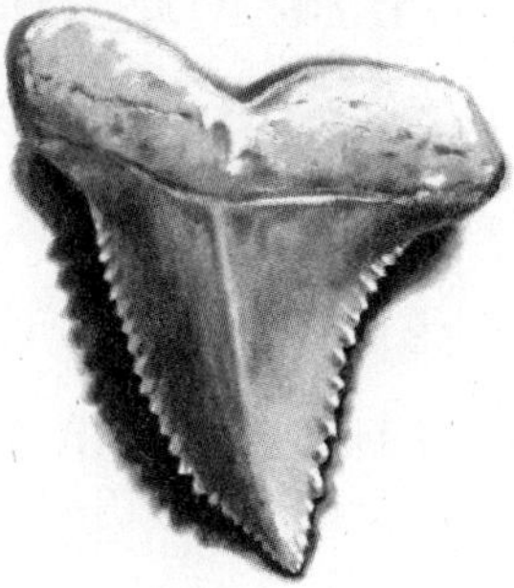

Chet rose to his knees and threw up.

When he could stand, he staggered over to his clothes. His hands were shaking so badly that he could barely button his shirt. He shoved his feet into his boots, not even trying to lace them. And then on wobbly legs, his blood pounding in his ears, he ran up the hill and found his way to Main Street.

He pushed past the ladies with their shopping baskets. He crossed the street, ignoring the honking motorcar that swerved around him. A man in a buggy shouted at him to watch out. The horse whinnied. Chet barely noticed.

He staggered into Mr. Colton's hardware store, tripping across the doorway and knocking over a display of watering cans. The clattering brought three customers to the front of the store. Mr. Colton hurried out from behind the counter.

"Chet?" he said worriedly. "What's wrong?"

Chet opened his mouth.

But he couldn't speak.

"What happened?" Mr. Colton said. "Why is your shirt covered with blood? Are you bleeding? Who did this to you?"

A small group of customers clustered around him, their eyes filled with concern.

Finally, Chet got the words out. "A shark."

"What?" Mr. Colton said.

"A shark," Chet repeated.

"Has there been another attack on the shore?"

Mr. Colton said. "I didn't see anything in the newspaper."

Chet shook his head.

"There's a shark in the creek," he said. "I saw it. It crashed into me."

The crowd erupted into loud laughter.

Mr. Colton offered a sympathetic smile and a hand on his shoulder. "It's the heat, my boy. It's driving us all a little mad."

He asked one of the customers to go into the back and bring Chet a drink. He led Chet through the laughing crowd and sat him on the stool behind the counter. A man handed Chet a tin mug of water.

"Take a drink, son," Mr. Colton said. But Chet pushed it away, and water splashed onto a pile of seed catalogs.

"We have to warn people!"

But Mr. Colton just shook his head, like Chet was a little kid who was sure he'd seen a unicorn galloping down the sidewalk.

"There's so much garbage floating in that creek," Mr. Colton said. "It could have been a plank from the dock, or a barrel, or a—"

"No," Chet said. "It was a shark!"

"I think maybe all those pranks are getting to you," Mr. Colton said.

Chet knew that he must sound crazy, that he could spend all day swearing that he'd seen a shark. Nobody would believe him.

Why would they?

A shark in the creek? It was impossible!

Except that Chet had seen it with his own eyes. If he'd been a step slower, he'd be dead right now, another name in the newspaper.

"It's all right, son," Mr. Colton said. "How about I call Dr. Jay and he'll give you a ride home. You've never been in his motorcar, have you?"

Mr. Colton headed to the back of the store to use the telephone.

The customers drifted away, shaking their heads and chuckling.

No, nobody would believe it. Meanwhile, that shark was still in the creek.

And then it hit Chet . . . that there was one person in town who just might believe him, who might know what to do. He wasn't sure, but it was his best hope.

He slid off the stool and rushed out of the store.

"Chet!" Mr. Colton called. "Where are you going?"

Chet didn't turn around.

He had to find Captain Wilson. He'd wasted enough time already.

CHAPTER 11

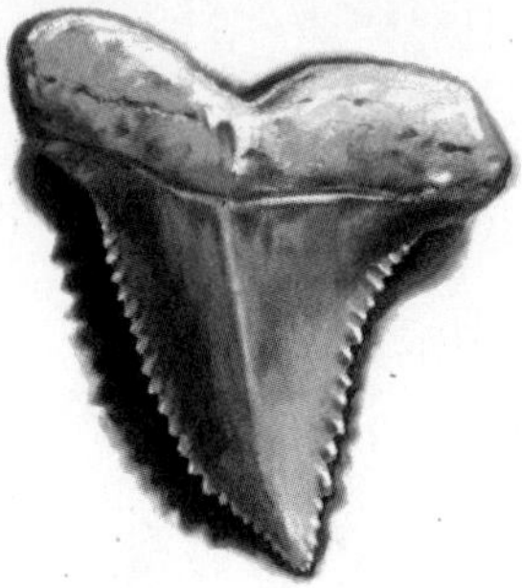

Chet stood on the sagging porch of the Captain's house. He'd barely knocked when the front door swung open.

The Captain stood there with a scowl on his crumpled-up face.

He looked at Chet like he'd never seen him before.

"Yes?" he said. "What is this about?"

Chet's heart sank.

He thought of what Uncle Jerry had said, that the Captain's mind was like Swiss cheese, full of holes and gaps in his memory.

"What is it?" the Captain said. "Are you selling something? I don't have all day."

"Sorry, sir," Chet said. "I didn't mean to bother you."

He almost turned around and walked away. But he forced himself to stay put. He stepped forward, close to the Captain, and peered right into his eyes.

"Captain," he said in a loud voice. "I saw a shark. In the creek. It crashed into me."

Chet lifted his shirt to show the angry-looking scrape.

The Captain stared at Chet's chest. Then he looked into the distance. Did he even know where he was?

"I know it sounds impossible, sir. It doesn't make any sense at all."

The Captain looked back at Chet. "Sure it does," he said.

Chet's eyes widened in surprise.

"The creek empties out into the Raritan Bay, which leads right to the Atlantic. Pirates used to come to these parts. Buried their treasure all around here."

The Captain's eyes kept getting brighter.

"If the tides are high, and the currents are strong, a shark could get swept right up into the creek."

Of course it could.

"I saw it, Captain," Chet said, more confident now. "It was huge. And its eyes, just like you said . . ."

"Killer eyes," the Captain muttered.

Chet nodded.

"Why are you standing here, son?" the Captain scolded. "We need to warn people! I'm getting my boat. You get down to that swimming hole. You tell people what you saw."

"What if they won't believe me?" Chet asked.

The Captain put a hand on Chet's shoulder. His grip was very strong.

"Go!" he said.

CHAPTER 12

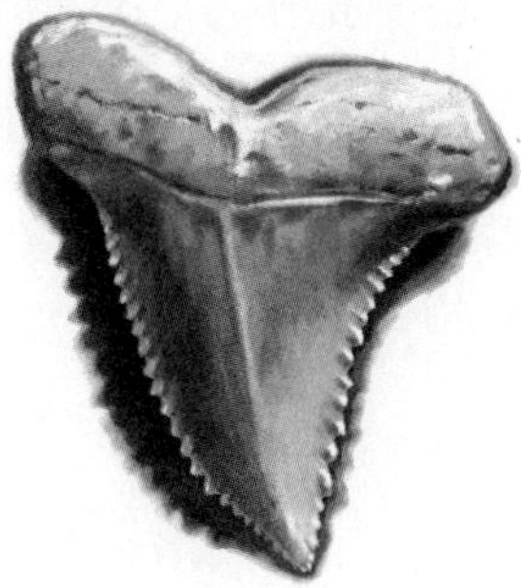

Chet started shouting halfway down the big hill. “Get out of the water!” he screamed. “Get out! Get out now!”

He thundered down the path and onto the dock. “You have to get out! There’s a shark!”

The guys were all there—but they didn’t even look at Chet.

“You have to believe me!” Chet insisted. “This isn’t a joke. You have to get out!”

"You hear that, Monty?" Sid said. "There's a shark in the creek! We better get out."

Sid hoisted himself up onto the dock, and Monty and Dewey followed.

Was it working? Were they listening?

But then Sid backed up and took a running leap off the edge of the dock. He cannonballed into the creek with such an enormous splash that Chet got drenched. Monty and Dewey dove in after him.

"Hey," Sid called. "If the shark attacks me, you guys can split the five-hundred-buck reward from that rich guy."

"That guy's dead!" Monty said.

"Too bad!" said Sid.

"Oh, shaaaaaaa-rrrrrrk!" Monty called through cupped hands. "Here, sharky shark! Come and get us!"

They hooted with laughter, and Chet stood there, totally helpless. That shark was probably long gone. Nobody would ever believe him. For the next hundred years, people around Elm Hills would be talking about Chet Roscow, the kid who had said there was a shark in the creek. He'd be a big joke, like the Captain was.

Chet felt like running away, far away. All the way to California.

But then he noticed Sid, strangely still in the creek. His face had gone white. His mouth was open, like he was going to scream.

Chet's insides turned to jelly when he saw the glistening fin moving slowly through the water.

"What the . . ." Dewey said.

"Hurry!" Chet cried. "Get out!"

Monty and Dewey flew out of the water.

But Sid seemed stuck, hypnotized.

The shark was closer to the surface now, its black eyes almost glowing. Its massive body looming.

They all screamed at Sid.

"Get out!"

"Hurry!"

"Come on! It's coming!"

Chet heard a motor in the distance, and Captain's Wilson's voice shouting, *"Shark! Shark in the creek! Everyone out! Shark in the creek!"*

Sid still didn't budge.

The shark was getting closer.

Suddenly, before he had a chance to think, Chet was in the water, swimming as fast as he

could toward Sid. He grabbed hold of Sid's arm and pulled him.

"Chet! Is it real?" Sid gasped. "Is it real?"

"Yes, yes, hurry!"

Monty and Dewey were at the edge of the dock, reaching down for them. Sid hoisted himself up, and Chet planted his hands on the dock. The guys all grabbed his arms to pull him up. Chet was almost out of the water when something caught his leg.

At first it felt like a giant hand was grabbing him. Then it felt like hot nails were boring into his calf.

"It's got my leg!" Chet screamed.

"Pull!" Sid shouted.

His friends pulled. They pulled and pulled until Chet was sure he'd be torn in two. After an eternity, his leg finally came free!

His friends hauled him onto the dock.

But then the shark exploded out of the water, its jaws wide open, its teeth smeared with blood. Its gaping mouth was coming right for Chet. And then —

BANG!

A gunshot shattered the air.

Time seemed to stop.

The next thing Chet knew, he was sitting on the dock. Everything looked foggy, and people seemed to be moving in slow motion. He heard muffled noises — men's voices, a boat's motor.

And the guys, saying his name over and over.

They were leaning close, still holding tight to his arms.

Chet looked down and wondered what he was doing in a puddle of ketchup. Hadn't he cleaned that up? Why was the puddle getting bigger?

Chet realized it wasn't the ketchup. It was blood pouring from his leg.

The fog around him grew thicker, until Chet couldn't see or hear a thing.

CHAPTER 13

SHARK KILLS TWO IN NEW JERSEY CREEK

A third boy survives, but injuries are grave

JULY 13, 1916

ELM HILLS, NEW JERSEY

A boy and a young man were killed yesterday, July 12, by a monster shark that made a shocking appearance in the Matawan Creek in New Jersey. Lester Stillwell, 11, was killed while swimming with friends in the town of Matawan. Minutes later, Stanley Fisher, 24, was killed as he bravely attempted to rescue young Lester.

Farther up the creek, Chet Roscow, 10, encountered the shark as he swam by himself. He managed to escape, and ran into town to alert residents. His cries of warning were ignored, with most residents dismissing his story as a prank. The boy did not give up, and later attempted to warn his friends, who were swimming behind the Templer Tile Factory. It was during these efforts that the lad fell into the jaws of the monstrous shark.

He was rescued moments later when Captain Thomas A. Wilson shot at the shark with a Civil War musket, scaring the beast away.

The brave youth was rushed to St. Peter's Hospital in New Brunswick. Injuries to his leg are described as extremely grave.

CHAPTER 14

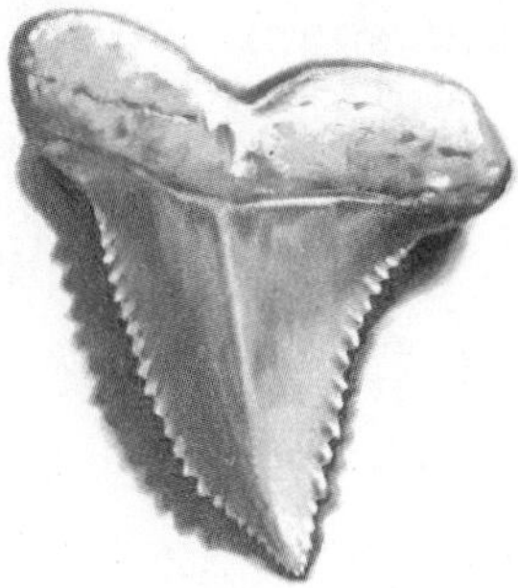

Pictures floated in and out of Chet's mind. Fuzzy pictures — men lifting him off the dock, the inside of Dr. Jay's motorcar, the white walls and white sheets of the hospital, unsmiling doctors shaking their heads, a pretty nurse with a soft voice. And Uncle Jerry, who always seemed to be sitting right next to Chet.

Was Chet asleep? Was he awake? Was he alive or was he dead?

It was two days before Chet decided for sure he was alive, and three more before he understood what had happened to him — that the shark had ripped away part of his calf. Another few seconds and that shark would have taken off his whole leg.

"It will heal," the doctor said, patting Chet on the shoulder. "It will take some time. But your leg will heal."

"The miracle kid," said Uncle Jerry. "That's what the newspapers are calling you. And it's true."

By then Chet had heard about the others — the boy attacked a mile down the creek from Elm Hills and the man who jumped in to try to save him. Both were dead.

Chet's room was filled with flowers and cards from people all over the country.

But none of it mattered to him. His leg hurt worse than it had when the shark was biting

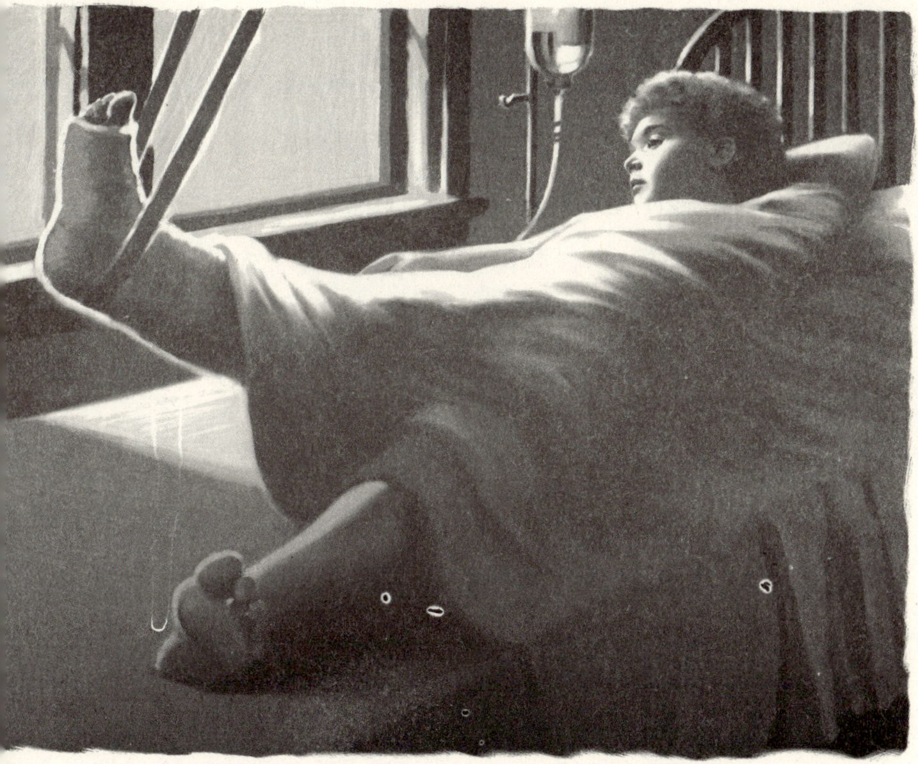

him. The medicine they gave him made him feel sick and woozy. He wanted Mama and Papa, but their train was still making its way across the country.

Every time Chet fell asleep, he woke up suddenly, shaking with fear, his bed soaked with sweat. The terror faded some when he was awake. But somehow that shark was always lurking. Its black killer eyes watching him, its bloody teeth glistening.

Chet had never felt so alone.

CHAPTER 15

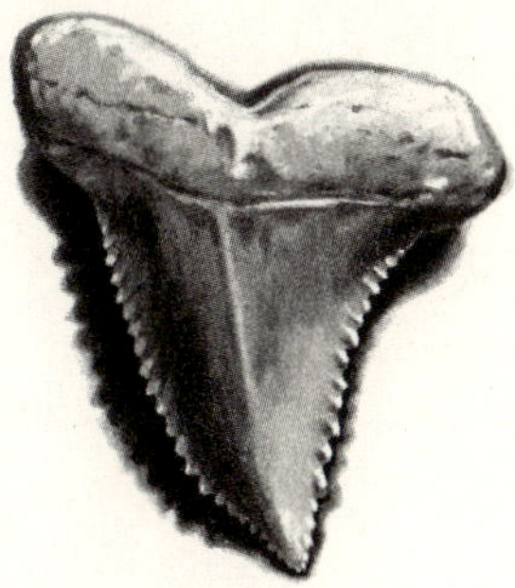

It was Chet's sixth morning in the hospital when there was a knock at his door. He sat up, sure it was Mama and Papa.

But it wasn't. Dewey, Sid, and Monty stood in the doorway. Uncle Jerry was right behind them. The hospital was a two-hour trip from Elm Hills. Had the guys really come all this way to see him?

They all looked a little scared, and Chet felt nervous. Were they still mad at him? Chet raised

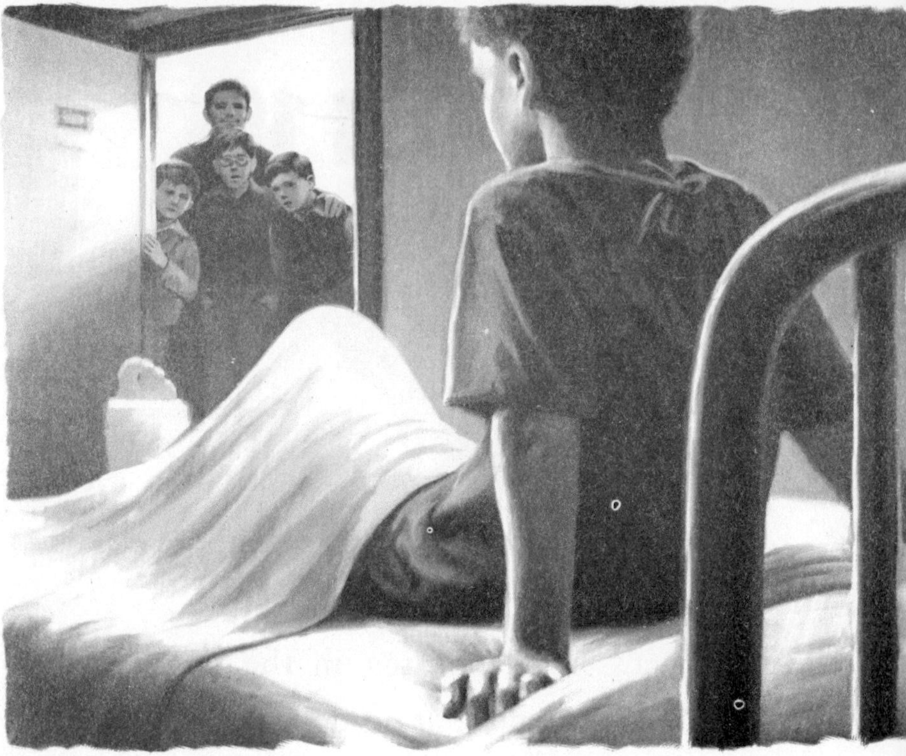

his hand and gave the briefest, tiniest wave. And just like that, the guys came barreling across the room, fighting each other for a spot on his little bed. Their jostling hurt his leg, but Chet couldn't have cared less.

"I'll be in the hallway, kiddo," Uncle Jerry said. "I think that pretty nurse likes me."

The door closed, and all the guys started talking at once.

"They dynamited the creek!"

"A guy caught a shark in the bay, says it's the same shark!"

"It was ten feet long!"

"They cut open its stomach."

"They found human bones!"

Of course Uncle Jerry had told Chet all this. But he didn't stop the guys from telling him again. He liked the sound of their voices around him. He hoped they never stopped talking. They told him that Captain Wilson was a celebrity, that newspaper reporters were coming from around the world to talk to him.

"Your uncle said your leg will be okay," Dewey said.

"You're going to have a huge scar," Sid said. He sounded almost jealous.

Chet hadn't looked too closely at his leg when the nurses changed his bandages. That was when it hurt the most, when they washed the wound. He had to keep his eyes closed tight and bite down on a rag to keep from screaming until the cleaning was done. A chunk of flesh was missing from his calf. He'd have more than a scar. He'd have a limp.

"Just like me," Uncle Jerry had said. "Won't slow you down a bit."

"Minnie keeps asking about you," Dewey said.

Chet wondered what Minnie would think of a boy with a limp.

Sid moved a little closer to Chet. "We're sorry," he whispered.

"We're sorry for everything," said Monty.

Sid looked like he was about to cry. "It's my fault."

"What?" Chet said. "You didn't put the shark in the creek."

Sid laughed a little, and wiped his eyes on his sleeve.

"We should have listened to you," Monty said. "If we had gotten out of the water, you wouldn't have gotten bitten."

"And if you hadn't come," Dewey said, "we'd be . . ."

"But if I hadn't played that stupid prank," Chet said, "you would have believed me."

"You saved me," Sid said.

"You guys saved *me*," Chet said. He swallowed hard, and they all sniffled a little.

Then a hush came over the room. And in that quiet moment, Chet realized something: He and the guys would always be tied together. By the terrible things they'd seen. By what they'd done for each other.

It was a while before Sid said, "We're calling a truce. No more pranks."

As usual, nobody argued with Sid. It was settled.

The guys stayed all afternoon, until Uncle Jerry poked his head in and said it was time to go. The guys lingered until Uncle Jerry shooed them out the door.

"Wait for me," Uncle Jerry told them, and then he closed the door and came over to Chet's bed.

"Your mama called the hospital," he said. "She and your papa will be here after dinner tonight."

Chet smiled.

"You know," Uncle Jerry said, straightening the sheet, "I had an idea, thought I'd mention it to you."

He cleared his throat.

"Maybe your papa would like to help me run the diner," Uncle Jerry said. "It's a busy place. I think he might enjoy it. We do well enough. And I sure wouldn't mind having more time to myself."

It took Chet a few seconds to understand what Uncle Jerry was saying.

"Your papa might decide it's time to settle

down," Uncle Jerry said. "I'm not sure he'll say yes, but I guess it's worth a try, don't you think?"

Chet opened his mouth to say something, but the words seemed to be all stuck together. So he just nodded.

"Okay then, kiddo. It's a plan."

Chet lay there a while after Uncle Jerry left. He thought about Mama and Papa. He couldn't wait to introduce them to the guys, and to Captain Wilson. He struggled to keep his eyes open, but it had been a long day. Before long he dozed off.

He dreamed that he was an old man, sitting in a diner, telling a story to a gang of boys. He told them about a shark in a creek, a huge killer shark with bloody jaws and coal-black eyes. He described how the shark had chased him, how it scared him out of his wits. But in the end, the beast couldn't get him. Because Chet hadn't been alone. Because his friends had reached out for him. They'd held him tight.

And they never let him go.

THE SHARK ATTACKS OF 1916: AN UNBELIEVABLE TRUE STORY

Imagine reading an article about a rabbit that suddenly turned into a bloodthirsty killer.

You would laugh, maybe, or shake your head in disbelief.

That's how most Americans in 1916 felt when they first heard about the shark attacks along the New Jersey shore. A shark attacking a human? Impossible! Sharks are tame creatures, most people believed, easily scared, with jaws too weak to do real damage to a human. There were no real marine biologists in those days, no scuba gear or submarines for underwater exploration. There had never been close studies of sharks, just stories passed down over generations. And of course everyone knew about Hermann Oelrichs and his famous reward: In 1891, the tycoon had offered $500 to anyone who could prove that a person had ever been attacked by a shark along the East Coast of the United States, north of North Carolina. Decades went by and nobody collected the reward. This seemed to confirm the popular belief that sharks posed no danger to humans.

And then came the attacks of 1916.

Though the characters in my book are made up, the major events of the story are true. Over twelve days during the scorching hot July of 1916, four people were killed in shark attacks. First Charles Vansant and then Charles Bruder were fatally wounded swimming in the ocean. Then, sixteen miles from the ocean, eleven-year-old Lester Stillwell was killed while he was swimming with his buddies in the Matawan Creek. Twenty-four-year-old Stanley Fisher was attacked trying to rescue Lester. Twelve-year-old Joseph Dunn was bitten on the leg but survived, just like Chet.

These attacks shocked America and shattered false ideas about sharks. There was no doubt that these were shark attacks. Two days after the Matawan attacks, a great white shark was caught in the Raritan Bay. It had human bones in its stomach, which seemed to prove that the killer had been caught.

But over the past few decades, scientists and investigators have raised questions about the attacks. Many doubt a lone great white was responsible. They say a bull shark is more likely to have attacked in the Matawan Creek, since that is the only man-eating species that can easily survive in fresh water for a length of time. In the weeks before the first attacks, ship captains had reported seeing more sharks than usual in the Atlantic shipping lanes, including great whites and bull sharks. Perhaps some unusual ocean or weather conditions had attracted sharks to the shore areas, where they tragically crossed paths with swimmers. We will never know for sure.

What we do know is that shark attacks are extremely rare.

And that the attacks of 1916 will never be forgotten.

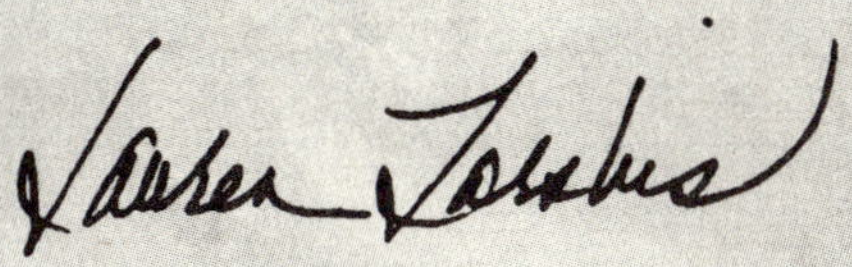

FACTS ABOUT SHARK ATTACKS

- Of the more than 350 known species of sharks, only 4 are particularly prone to attack a human: the bull shark, the great white, the tiger shark, and the hammerhead. The bull shark is considered by many experts to be the most dangerous to humans.
- Shark attacks are very rare. In 2008, there were 118 attacks reported worldwide, and 4 deaths. Of those attacks, 59 were "unprovoked," which means that the shark attacked someone who was not doing anything to deliberately attract or touch it. In contrast, an average of 125,000 people die of snakebites each year.

- Some scientists believe that most sharks don't mean to attack humans, but mistake surfers or swimmers for large sea mammals, like seals. This could explain why most shark attacks on humans are not fatal — a shark takes one bite, realizes its mistake, and swims away.
- Most shark attacks happen to people swimming alone in the ocean. Experts suggest that the best way to avoid an attack is to swim in groups. Other tips: Avoid swimming at night or at dusk. Swimming with a dog can be dangerous, because the whirling motion of the dog's paws in the water can attract sharks. Leave jewelry at home, since bright objects can also attract sharks. And don't swim in the ocean if you have a bleeding wound.

- Florida is the number-one shark-attack state, with an average of thirty attacks a year. There have been no deaths over the past four years. California, Hawaii, North Carolina, and South Carolina have had a few attacks over the last five years. There has not been another attack recorded in New Jersey since 1926.
- Every year, humans kill nearly 100 million sharks, mainly for their fins, which are a prized ingredient for shark fin soup. Many shark species are endangered, including the great white.
- The International Shark Attack File investigates every reported shark attack in the world and maintains detailed records. Check out their fascinating website: http://www.flmnh.ufl.edu/fish/

Can you survive another thrilling story based on true events?

Read on for a sneak peek at

I SURVIVED

HURRICANE KATRINA, 2005

Cleo threw up all day. Barry tried to help keep her calm. But even he couldn't get her to stop crying. Mom managed to talk to their doctor, who had evacuated. He said there was a bad stomach flu going around, and that Cleo wouldn't start to feel better until tomorrow.

Mom and Dad talked about going to the Superdome. But the news reports said there were already ten thousand people at the stadium, and more people lined up around the building. They decided with Cleo still sick, they were better off at home.

All afternoon, Barry stepped out on the porch to look at the sky.

It was windier than usual, and the sky was a dark gray streaked with silver. But the strangest thing was the silence. Their block was deserted.

There were no motorcycles vrooming. No kids laughing and shouting. No music playing or basketballs bouncing. Usually the trees were filled with birds, and frogs chirped from the bushes. But there wasn't a bird in sight, and not a peep to be heard.

And then, at around 10:00 that night, the winds and rain started up for real.

Dad and Barry were settled on the living room couch. The baseball playoffs were on. Mom and Cleo were fast asleep.

The wind whispered at first. Then it started to whistle, and moan, and finally it was shrieking so loudly Dad had to turn up the TV. Barry moved closer to Dad.

Soon there were other noises.

Pom, pom, pom.

"That's just the rain banging against the metal roof on the shed," Dad said.

Kabang!

"I think a gutter came loose."

Chechong!

"There goes part of someone's fence."

Dad clicked off the TV. He reached over and grabbed his trumpet, which he always kept close by.

The wind shrieked a high note. Dad put his trumpet to his lips and played along.

The wind shifted lower, and so did Dad.

He played softly, along with the wind, until after a while that wind didn't seem so scary, until it actually sounded like a song. The house shook and rattled, but as Dad's music filled the air, Barry started to feel safe. The lights were bright. Mom and Cleo were cozy in their beds. In a few hours the sky would turn blue again.

Barry closed his eyes. . . . drifting, drifting, drifting . . .

And then his eyes popped open.

It took Barry a minute to understand that he had fallen asleep. The room was dark except for a candle flickering on the corner table. The power must have gone out. He squinted at his watch: 4:35. He'd slept for hours.

And something woke him up. A noise. Not the wind, which was still shrieking and moaning. Not the rain, which hammered down even harder than when Barry closed his eyes. No. There was a new noise out there. A kind of whooshing sound.

Barry sat up. How long had he slept?

Where was Dad? And what was that strange noise that had woken Barry up?

Barry heard Dad's footsteps upstairs. He stood up, but before he could take two steps the front door flew open.

A wave of water swept into the house. It swirled around Barry's legs, knocking him off his feet.

There was a shrieking sound, but this time it wasn't the wind that was screaming.

It was Barry.

Dad was pounding down the stairs. He splashed through the water, grabbed Barry by the arm, lifting him up, and pulled him towards the stairs. Furniture floated around them—the new couch Mom saved for a year to buy, the little square lamp table where Gramps used to play chess, framed pictures of Barry and Cleo from school—all floating like bath toys. The water was rising so fast! It was up to Barry's waist by the time they reached the stairs—and it kept getting higher and higher. It was like their house was a bucket being filled up by the biggest hose in the world.

Where was all this water coming from?

Mom burst out of her room with Cleo in her arms.

She looked down the stairs and gasped. She wrapped her free arm around Barry, pulling him close.

"The levee, Roddy," she said to Dad.

Dad nodded. "The canal."

"The levee broke?" Barry said, picturing the Industrial Canal a block and a half from their house. It was a football field wide, and so deep that barges could go through. Was all that water pouring into their neighborhood?

Mom and Dad seemed frozen there, staring at the rising water.

Panic boiled up inside Barry.

"What will happen?" Barry said. "What will we do? What. . . " he trailed off, not even sure what he wanted to ask.

They all stood there, huddled together, watching the water rise up the stairs.

"We need to go up to the attic," Dad said. "Now."

Dad pulled open the hatch in the ceiling and a blast of hot air came down. Barry had only been up there once in his life. It was a tiny space, dark and hot like an oven, with a ceiling that sloped down so you couldn't stand up straight.

Cleo started to cry.

"No!" she said. She started to run. "No go up!"

Dad caught her. "Cleo!" he said. She struggled to escape, screaming and squirming. There was no way they could force her up the rickety stairs.

"It's all right," Barry managed to say, taking hold of his sister's hand.

Dad sent Mom up first. Then Barry put Cleo on the ladder, and climbed right behind her. Dad came last, and they all sat down together in the hot darkness. There was barely enough room for the four of them, and they were all squashed together. The air was so hot it burned Barry's lungs. It stank like mildew and dust.

He tried not to imagine what was happening just below the attic floor — that every single thing they owned — their furniture, their beds, Cleo's toys, Mom's cookbooks, Dad's trumpet and all of his music — was covered with water.

With every minute that ticked by, Barry felt more helpless and terrified. Cleo was whimpering again. Mom held her on her lap, rocking back and forth, singing softly to calm her.

The water was rising through the second floor. They could hear it moving furniture around through the open attic door.

What would they do? Where could they go?

His whole body was shaking.

What would happen to them? How would they escape?

And then Dad put one hand on Barry's shoulder and the other on Mom's.

"I want you to listen carefully," he said, his voice low and calm. "We are all together. And as long as we're all together, we are going to come through this."

Even in the darkness, Barry could see Dad's eyes blazing.

"In a few hours this will be over," Dad said. "We just have to get through the next few hours."

Mom wiped away Barry's tears.

"We can't stay here in the attic," Dad said. "We're going up onto the roof."

Mom's eyes got wider. She swallowed. "All right," she said.

"But there's no way out," Barry said.

"Yes, there is," Dad said.

Dad made his way to the corner of the attic. He came back with what looked like a stick.

As he got closer, Barry saw what it was: an ax.

"Gramps always said there'd be another bad storm," Dad said. "He kept this ax up here for forty years. And he made sure I knew about it."

It took Barry a minute to understand what Dad was doing to do with that ax.

"Keep the kids back," Dad said to Mom.

Mom had pulled Barry and Cleo against the back wall. She stood over them, her arms spread out like a shield.

Dad heaved the ax over his shoulder. With a mighty swing, he smashed the blade into the ceiling.